Acknowledgements

All praise belongs to Allah alone, and may Allah's blessings
and peace be upon Muhammad and upon his family,
descendants, and companions.

I dedicate this book to my niece, Alyssa, who inspired it.
One day, we were talking about the things that we like and
Alyssa remarked "a totally chocolate world would be fun."

ISBN 978-0-86037-408-4

MUSLIM CHILDREN'S LIBRARY

Amira's Totally Chocolate World
Author: J. Samia Mair
Editor: Farah Alvi
Illustrations: Craigh Howarth
Book Design: Nasir Cadir
Coordinator: Anwar Cara

Published by:
THE ISLAMIC FOUNDATION,
Markfield Conference Centre, Ratby Lane, Markfield,
Leicestershire, LE67 9SY, United Kingdom
Website: www.islamic-foundation.com

QURAN HOUSE, P.O. Box 30611, Nairobi, Kenya

P.M.B. 3193, Kano, Nigeria

All enquiries to: Kube Publishing
Tel: +44(0)1530 249230, Fax +44(0)1530 249656
Email: info@kubepublishing.com www.kubepublishing.com

A catalogue record of this book is available from the British Library

Amira's Totally Chocolate World

J. Samia Mair

Illustrated by Craigh Howarth

One day while Amira was sitting in her garden and eating a chocolate candy bar she had an idea – a great idea! Wouldn't it be wonderful if the whole world were made of chocolate? Wouldn't it be wonderful if it were a totally chocolate world!

Amira thought of all the fun things that she would do in a totally chocolate world. She would pick chocolate flowers from her garden and eat them. She would run through the chocolate grass and occasionally reach down to taste it. She would open her mouth to the sky when it rained and drink droplets of delicious chocolate. Best of all, she would sail on waves of dark creamy chocolate, drinking glasses of chocolate all day long. Amira thought, "What a wonderful world a totally chocolate world would be!"

The more and more Amira thought about a totally chocolate world, the happier she became. Every night before she went to sleep, Amira closed her eyes and asked Allah for a totally chocolate world. Every morning when she woke up, however, the flowers still smelled liked flowers; the grass still felt like grass; the rain still tasted like rain; and the ocean near her home was still blue.

One night, Amira felt excited when going to bed because the next day was a very special day. It was Eid ul-Fitr. This was the first Ramadan that Amira had fasted for a part of each day. Her mother had promised to bake a special chocolate cake with thick chocolate icing, especially for her.

Amira woke up the next morning and looked out of her window to admire her garden. Usually, her garden had big pink roses, bright yellow daisies, purple petunias, and orange lilies. The grass was soft and green and jasmine filled the air with its sweet aroma.

But when she looked out of her window this day, an amazing surprise waited for her. Everything was chocolate – the flowers, the grass, the trees, everything! Amira thought, "Today *is* a very very special day."

Amira quickly got dressed and ran outside to see her totally chocolate world. She picked a flower from her garden and bit it. Chocolate never tasted so good.

She reached down and grabbed several blades of chocolate grass. They were just as sweet. Amira felt little drops fall on her head and looked up. It was raining chocolate! She opened her mouth to the sky and let it fill with the delicious chocolate falling from above.

When the chocolate rain stopped, a chocolate rainbow appeared in the sky. It was made of dark brown chocolate, light brown chocolate, white chocolate, and four other shades of chocolate. Amira then remembered what she had wanted most of all – waves of dark creamy chocolate.

She ran through the chocolate fields and the chocolate forest that led to the ocean. She climbed over the chocolate sand dunes and raced across the chocolate sand until the water's edge. Foamy, dark chocolate waves crashed on the shore, making the most delicious sound.

Amira scooped up a handful of the chocolate ocean and sipped it. It was just as wonderful as she had imagined. Amira jumped into her sailboat and sailed on chocolate waves, drinking cups and cups of chocolate all day long.

16

Amira then remembered that it was Eid and that her family would be worried if she did not return home soon. She sailed quickly back to shore and ran through the chocolate forest and chocolate fields as fast as she could. As she approached the front door of her house, Amira noticed her garden. The smell of jasmine did not fill the air. The brown chocolate grass did not feel soft on her feet. She missed the beautiful colours.

17

Amira thought, "Maybe it wouldn't be too bad if roses were pink and daisies were yellow and petunias were purple and lilies were orange. Maybe it wouldn't be too bad if grass were soft and green. Maybe it wouldn't be too bad if jasmine smelled like jasmine."

Amira had many other thoughts as well. If roses were pink and daisies were yellow, and if petunias were purple and lilies were orange, and if grass were green and jasmine smelled like jasmine, rain would have to be rain. Everybody knows flowers and plants need water to grow. And while a chocolate ocean is wonderful, a blue ocean is special too.

"What a wonderful world a world of different colours would be!" Amira thought, recalling the ayat in the Qur'an that mention the many colours of creation. Amira closed her eyes and made another du'a, this time asking Allah to return the world back to the way He had created it.

Amira's alarm clock rang so loudly that she jumped out of bed.
She ran to her window. She saw big pink roses, bright yellow
daisies, purple petunias, and orange lilies. The grass looked
soft and green. The scent of jasmine seeped through the open
window, filling her room with its sweet aroma.

"*Al-Hamdulillah*!" she exclaimed. Amira realized that she had only dreamt about a totally chocolate world. She thought, "Today *is* a very, very special day, indeed. What a beautiful world I live in – a world of different colours." Amira whispered softly, "*Subhanallah*, all praise and thanks belong to Allah our Creator, the All-wise and the All-knowing."

22

Amira ran to find her mother. She wanted to tell her mother about her dream and the lessons that she had learned from it. On the kitchen table she found a large chocolate cake with thick chocolate icing, baked especially for her.

Al-Hamdulillah – Praise belongs to Allah.

Ayat – Verses in the Qur'an; 'Ayat' is the plural of 'ayah'.

Du'a – A prayer in which we ask something good from Allah.

Eid ul-Fitr – "The Festival of Fast-Breaking"; Eid ul-Fitr is the celebration that begins on the first day of Shawwal, the tenth month in the Islamic lunar calendar which follows Ramadan.

Qur'an – The Holy Book of the Muslims, revealed to the Prophet Muhammad.

Ramadan – The ninth month in the Islamic lunar calendar, during which Muslims fast from dawn to sunset.

Subhanallah – Glory be to Allah.

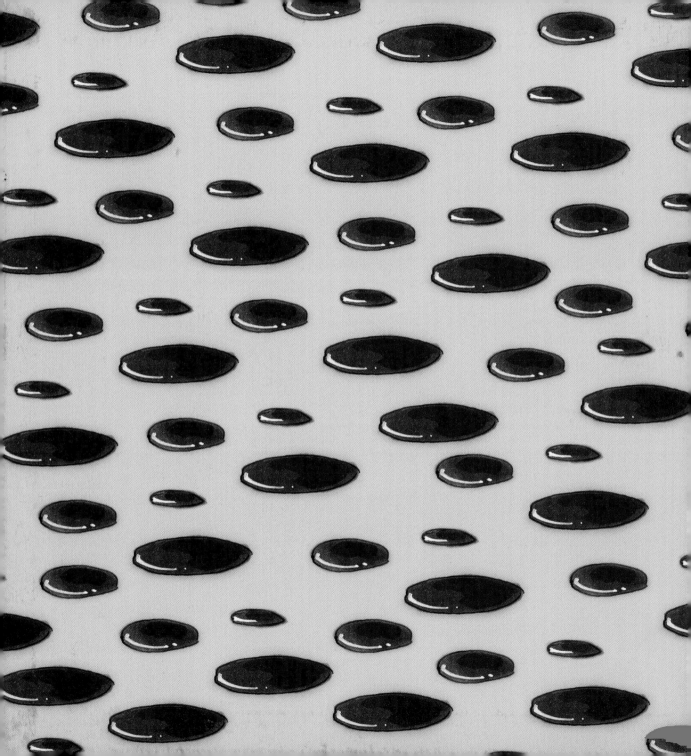